Peppa's School Day

Adapted by Meredith Rusu

SCHOLASTIC INC.

This book is based on the TV series *Peppa Pig*. *Peppa Pig* is created by Neville Astley and Mark Baker.
Peppa Pig © Astley Baker Davies Ltd/Entertainment One UK Ltd 2003.

ISBN 978-1-338-32785-4

10 9 8 7 6 5 4 3 2 1   18 19 20 21 22

Printed in the U.S.A.   40
First printing September 2018

Peppa is going to school today.

All of her friends are there!

"Today we have a new
student," says Madame Gazelle.
"This is Emily Elephant."

Emily is shy.
She does not know what to say.

Everyone is excited to meet Emily!

"Can I show Emily how we do show-and-tell?" Peppa asks.

"Of course," says Madame Gazelle.

Peppa tells the class about her teddy bear.

Next, it is free time.

"What would you like to do
today?" Peppa asks Emily.

There is painting, clay, or building blocks.

Emily chooses building blocks!

Peppa shows Emily how to
stack the blocks.

"You put one on top of another," says Peppa.

"Like this?" asks Emily.
"Wow!" say the children.

Emily Elephant is good at stacking blocks!

Next, it is playtime!
"Come on, Emily," shouts
Peppa.

"At playtime, we go outside!"
says Candy Cat.

All the children run outside.

First, they go down the slide.

Wheeeee!

Then they play a game.
"Who is the loudest?" asks
Peppa. *Snort!*

They all make loud sounds.
What a lot of noise!

Erowrrhhh!!

"Emily, you try," says Peppa.
Emily makes a noise like a
trumpet.

She is the loudest of all!

"Can you spin the hula hoop?" Suzy Sheep asks Emily.

Emily can spin the hula hoop.
She is good at lots of things!

But there is still one game left to play.

"My favorite game is jumping in muddy puddles," says Peppa. "That is my favorite game, too!" shouts Emily.

Peppa and Emily are so happy
they are friends.
What a nice day at school!